BRAVE DEEDS

BRAVE
DEEDS

How One Family Saved Many from the Nazis

ANN ALMA

GROUNDWOOD BOOKS
HOUSE OF ANANSI PRESS
TORONTO BERKELEY

j 940.5318
alma

Groundwood Books / House of Anansi Press
110 Spadina Avenue, Suite 801, Toronto, Ontario M5V 2K4
or c/o Publishers Group West
1700 Fourth Street, Berkeley, CA 94710

We acknowledge for their financial support of our publishing program the Canada Council for the Arts, the Government of Canada through the Book Publishing Industry Development Program (BPIDP) and the Ontario Arts Council.

 ONTARIO ARTS COUNCIL
CONSEIL DES ARTS DE L'ONTARIO

 BRITISH COLUMBIA ARTS COUNCIL
We acknowledge the support of the Province of British Columbia through the British Columbia Arts Council

Library and Archives Canada Cataloguing in Publication
Alma, Ann
Brave deeds : how one family saved many from the Nazis / Ann Alma.
ISBN-13: 978-0-88899-791-3
ISBN-10: 0-88899-791-4
1. Braal family–Juvenile literature. 2. World War, 1939-1945–Jews–Rescue–Netherlands–Juvenile literature. 3. World War, 1939-1945–Children–Netherlands–Juvenile literature. 4. World War, 1939-1945–Underground movements–Netherlands–Juvenile literature. 5. Netherlands–History–German occupation, 1940-1945–Juvenile literature. 6. Righteous Gentiles in the Holocaust–Netherlands–Biography–Juvenile literature. I. Title.
DJ283.B73A45 2008   j940.53'18350922492   C2007-907130-9

Cover photographs:
(Front top) Hulton Archive / Getty Images
(Front bottom and back) Braal family archives

Design by Michael Solomon
Printed and bound in Canada

To Frans and Mies Braal,
the memories of your brave deeds live on.

CONTENTS

CHAPTER 1
ROTTERDAM,
THE NETHERLANDS,
AUTUMN 1944

I wake up when something touches my face. The bedroom is black, the night's silence as brittle as wafers. Mama bends over me and kisses my forehead, her warm hands cradling my cheeks.

"Your papa and I need to go into hiding for a while, lieveling," she whispers. "Our friend, the man with the black beard, is waiting for you. Go with him. He will keep you safe."

Papa pulls her back. "Hurry," he says urgently. He doesn't explain why he and Mama have to leave. Papa doesn't say much anymore. Not since the Nazis blew up his fishing boat, and he and Mama started doing dangerous resistance jobs.

I'm still struggling to shake the sleep from my head when heavy trucks screech to a stop beneath the bedroom window. Men yell in German. My body turns into a cold hard lump of clay.

The Nazis hit and kick the front door. Papa picks

Frans Braal, or Oom Frans, was the leader of the Dutch Resistance Movement in the town of Oostvoorne on the island of Voorne.

me up, blankets, sheet and all. He slips me over his shoulder. I know I am light, even if I am eleven years old. We climb out the back hall window, slide down the short steep roof and run along the alley. Mama runs beside us, a small suitcase in her hand.

At the end of the alley I see the man with the black beard. He's straddling a bicycle, ready to ride off down the dark streets. Setting me on the bicycle's back carrier,

Papa quickly kisses my cheeks, first one, then the other.

"Be brave," he whispers.

As we ride away I watch Papa and Mama running down another alley. Soon blackness swallows them up. I want to call after them. But I don't. Instead I hold on tightly to the man with the beard.

We move off into the night. We ride and ride until finally we leave the streets of Rotterdam behind. The man stops when we get to a clump of trees. He leans on the handlebars, breathing hard from pedaling so fast.

"We have to bike for a few more hours," he says. "We're going to Het Buitenhuis, on Voorne. That's where I live. My name is Frans Braal but you can call me Oom Frans. My wife, Tante Mies, will have a bed for you. There will be other children for you to play with. You'll be safe."

"Where are Papa and Mama going?" I ask, my voice trembling.

"You know I can't tell you," he says. "They're going to a safe place. The war will be over soon and then they'll come back to get you."

CHAPTER 2
HET BUITENHUIS

At Het Buitenhuis there are many, many different people — Oom Frans and Tante Mies and their children Wiese, Marjan and Frank. There's Tante Toos and her daughter, Rita. And then there are the people in hiding — Peter and Reinder, who are close to my age, Mrs. Reyne and Mrs. Laroy, who help Tante Mies, and a lot of other people whose names I don't know.

I don't know why all these people are in hiding. Sometimes new people come, and then they leave again. None of us know who they are. We don't ask any questions. If we don't know them, we can't spill their secrets.

I've been at this country place for almost two weeks now and I want to go home. I want to know where Papa and Mama are. Oom and Tante won't tell me, so I try to listen in on their conversations. I've become a sleuth.

Yesterday I overheard Tante Mies telling one of the new people that Oom Frans is a member of the Dutch Resistance Movement, like Papa and Mama. Oom doesn't believe in war. Even before the Nazis invaded the Netherlands he told the Dutch government that he was a conscientious objector. He told them he would never carry weapons or kill people. He wants to work for peace instead.

This morning Oom and Tante sit side by side on a bench in the woods of Het Buitenhuis. Their backs are turned to me, their faces soaking up the fall sunshine. I'm crouched in a dry ditch right behind them.

Het Buitenhuis, or the house out in the country, was big enough to hide a number of people. It was a rectangular building with one large central common room and a kitchen. A door on each side of the common room led to a dormitory with ten bunk beds and two smaller bedrooms. The house was secluded and was surrounded by trees, farms and market gardens.

Although the tall weeds rustle a little in the breeze, if I stay very still I can hear them.

"The Nazis have taken Reverend van der Meer to one of their bunkers." Even when Oom whispers, his voice is powerful.

"Do you think they'll make him talk?" Tante's voice is much quieter. I have to strain to hear her.

"Maybe. Van der Meer knows..."

A noisy seagull flies overhead, drowning out Oom's words for a few seconds.

"...no telling what they'll do," he continues. "The soldiers came looking for his radio. I told him it wasn't safe." Oom Frans smacks his hands down on his thighs. "He knows the Nazis have forbidden radios. He was listening to the BBC when they arrived!"

"Shhhh," Tante says. "The children might hear you."

Mies Braal, or Tante Mies, took care of her own family as well as everyone else at Het Buitenhuis.

My body tightens. Papa and Mama had a radio hidden under the floor. Did the Nazis find out that they printed leaflets of what they heard on the news? Is that why they went into hiding?

Oom Frans has a radio too. Will the Nazis come here to arrest him?

"What will happen?" Tante asks.

"If Van der Meer breaks under their interrogation, he might tell secrets about the resistance," Oom says. "He knows an awful lot. I take stolen ration cards and coupons to him all the time. I'd better go into hiding for a few days until things settle down. I'll take *him* with me."

Oom means he's taking one of our biggest secrets — the man we're never allowed to talk about — the Canadian airman who fell from a burning plane in the sky.

When the Nazis shot the Canadian's plane down he floated to the ground in his parachute. He had burns on his body and had hurt his ankle.

First he cut off the tops of his army boots and the insignia on his uniform and hid them, along with his parachute, in a swamp. Then he managed to hobble to a nearby farm. The farmer was afraid to let him in and sent him away. But at the next farm, the family hid him in the loft of their barn until they could contact the resistance movement. They were too afraid to hide him in the house.

Oom Frans went to get the airman, taking an extra bicycle with him. Then the two men set off for Oom

Frans's house. The Canadian followed at a safe distance so that if the Nazis stopped him, Oom would be able to get away.

When they arrived, Oom told Tante who the stranger was and asked her if they could hide him. "Yes, of course," Tante Mies said. "Sit down and have a cup of tea." Oom gave the Canadian airman some of his clothes to wear. He also gave him a Dutch name — Henk Poldervaart.

At that time Oom and Tante lived right in the town of Oostvoorne. Tante started to worry that it was too dangerous for her family, with their three little children, to have a twenty-four-year-old stranger who couldn't speak Dutch staying at their home. People would begin to ask questions like, "Who is that young man staying at the Braals' place?" "Where did he come from?" "Why doesn't he ever say anything?" So Oom and Tante traded their nice, cozy house for Het Buitenhuis.

If the Nazis find out that a downed airman is hiding here, they will take him to a prisoner-of-war camp and interrogate him. Oom and Tante will be shot.

Oom Frans yawns loudly and stretches. He didn't get much sleep last night because he was out doing resistance work. When I close one eye, I can see him with my other one through a little opening in the tall grass.

Oom stares off into the distance, his hands in the pockets of his knickerbockers, his checkered knee socks stretching over his calf muscles. Even though he's a short man, he's strong and fit from riding his bicycle. He rakes his fingers through his unruly thick black

The Canadian airman, Philip Pochailo, gives Wiese, Marjan and baby Frank a ride. Downed airmen were usually smuggled back to their air bases in England within a few days of landing. "The Canadian" was at first too injured, then too sick to travel. By the time he was well enough, the secret route to England had been closed due to heavy fighting between the Nazis and the Allied soldiers. The Braals hid him at Het Buitenhuis for seven months.

hair. I smile when I think of how Papa always called Oom "our black-bearded little giant." Tante says the Nazis call him Jesus.

Oom reaches a hand out to Tante who groans as she stands up because she's very pregnant. She waddles back and forth with her hands around her belly.

"We'll go right away," Oom says. "It's better if I don't tell you exactly where. Send the signal when it seems safe for us to come home."

I know Oom and the Canadian can't get off this island together. Nazi soldiers guard the Spijkenisse

The Spijkenisse bridge, patrolled by Nazi guards, connected the island of Voorne to the mainland.

bridge day and night because they built their bunkers all along the coast. The bridge is too dangerous for the Canadian to cross. But Oom can leave the island when he's by himself. He works for the water board, so he has a travel pass.

When Oom and Tante have gone, I leave my hiding place. My legs hurt from crouching so long in the ditch and, like Tante, I groan as I stand up.

A thick gray fog has rolled in and the sun has disappeared. It's often misty here because we're so close to the North Sea. I shiver as cold wet fog fingers slowly slide across my bare face, arms and legs.

Tante Mies will be tense and quiet while Oom is in hiding. She thinks we don't notice, and maybe the little ones don't. The adults try to hide their worry from all us children at Het Buitenhuis. But I can feel her fear. I wish the war was over.

I don't know Tante Mies's signal for when it's safe for Oom and the Canadian to return. I'll find out though. The more I know, the more I feel safe. But some days the more I know, the more I feel scared.

CHAPTER 3
THE HIDING CUPBOARD

After three days and two nights Oom Frans and the Canadian come out of hiding. They are exhausted, dirty, just about frozen and absolutely starving. They hid in a ditch somewhere in the woods. They stayed there the whole time.

Tante Mies makes them large helpings of hot stamppot, with potatoes, carrots, onions, milk and salt. She has no sausages or butter right now. They share one hard-boiled duck egg, even though eggs are incredibly expensive. One of Tante's friends gave it to her yesterday.

Oom Frans and the Canadian almost fall asleep over their stamppot. After they finish, Tante Mies and Tante Toos put us kids to bed.

I can't sleep. I've become a night owl. Bomber planes fly overhead every night, hundreds and hundreds of them. The droning goes on and on, like millions of giant killer bees in a constant swarm. They give me nightmares.

So when the women have gone back to the common room I leave my bed and crawl into my hiding cupboard. It's full of towels and facecloths and Tante's sewing things. The space is small and a bit cramped, but I feel safe here. Tante's sewing things are just like Mama's.

The cupboard has two doors, one to the dorm and one to the common room. When I crouch down I can see my dorm through a little knothole in the wall. If I turn carefully, I can see into the common room through a crack between the wall and the cupboard door.

The adults are at the far end of the common room playing charades and laughing loudly. Tante Mies and Oom Frans leave the game and walk toward me.

Do they know I'm hidden here?

They stop in front of the cupboard. Oom Frans leans against the wall, listening. Tante tells him that their friend Pieter Langendoen came over today and helped her bury the radio in the manure pile. Pieter told her it wasn't safe to keep it in the house any longer, not after what happened to van der Meer.

The Canadian is the one in Het Buitenhuis who listened to the radio the most, to hear the latest BBC news. He lived in England for a year so that he could become a flying officer and be trained as a bombardier. I don't like him. Maybe because he dropped bombs from a plane, even if they weren't meant for the Dutch people. Or maybe because he speaks a different language. He scares me.

Reverend van der Meer often invited friends over to listen to the radio and he hid other people's radios for them. His house was raided by the Nazis who interrogated and then shot him because he refused to give them any information about other resistance workers, including the Braals. After the war a street in Oostvoorne was named in his honor.

Tante Mies is teaching him to speak Dutch, but he sounds kind of funny when he tries. I laugh when I hear him, although I don't let Tante see or she'd scold me for being rude. Now the Canadian can crawl under the manure pile to listen to the news! I'd better never say that out loud. Everybody else here likes him a lot.

Then Tante Mies tells Oom Frans that Reverend van der Meer was shot. Oom's face becomes so sad and stern, he has to look away. Tante Mies strokes his arm and says that she's glad Oom is safe and that the radio is gone, even if hearing the news gave them so much hope. She says that the war will be over soon because the Allied troops have already freed parts of France, Belgium and the most southern parts of Holland.

Oom still looks worried.

"The Allies tried to free Arnhem but it was a disaster," he says. "So was our railway strike. We may have to hide some of the strikers. We'd better prepare for another long cold winter. People have nothing to eat."

Tante Mies tells Oom Frans he is overtired and he'd best get some sleep.

I want to stay here, in this warm cupboard. The women will come to check all us children, but my bed has my pillow and my clothes bunched up under the blankets and the sheet pulled up to the top.

They always let me sleep with my head under the blankets. They know the sound of the planes scares me, even though all the windows are blacked out with paper so the planes that fly over can't see any lights down below. That way the pilots won't know where the villages and cities are. The blacked-out windows make the dorm so dark, the women won't notice that I'm not in my bed.

I must have fallen asleep for a while too, right here on the towels and facecloths. Now I'm wide awake again. Noises from outside reach my ears. They are not the regular nighttime sounds.

"Wo ist er denn?" a voice yells.

"Where is he?" That's what those German words mean. Nazi soldiers are outside. They are not looking for the radio. They are looking for the Canadian! Did somebody tell the Nazis about our secret? My body freezes.

Suddenly the door to the dorm opens noiselessly. Just a tiny bit of light comes in. I hold my breath. It's Tante Mies. She usually sleeps in one of the small

Allied pilots flew bombing missions from England over Holland to Germany. They flew their Avro Lancaster bombers under the cover of darkness in formations of hundreds, even thousands of planes. Each heavy bomber carried a crew of seven or eight, consisting of a pilot, a flight engineer, a navigator and wireless operator, a bombardier and several air gunners.

rooms at the far end of the other dorm — the dorm where most of the people who are in hiding sleep, the end where the noises are coming from.

Tante waddles over to Oom Frans. He's asleep on a bottom bunk, the Canadian above him. Tante shakes him.

"Frans, de Duitsers, de Duitsers!" she whispers. She shakes him harder. I keep one eye glued to the knot-hole. I'm afraid I'm going to throw up. I hold my mouth clamped shut with one hand and my stomach with the other.

Finally, Oom Frans is awake. Tante whispers that the Nazis are outside with flashlights. I whirl around in the cupboard, but of course the common-room windows are blacked out too. Tante must have opened her little bedroom window to see what was happening.

Oom jumps out of bed and roughly shakes the Canadian.

"The others have already left," Tante says. "The Germans are searching the shed. Don't go there."

The two men run out the back door without even getting dressed.

Tante Mies grabs their warm blankets and spreads them over the smallest sleeping children. She yanks the sheets off their beds and, together with the men's clothes, stuffs them in to the bottom of the laundry hamper. Then she turns Oom Frans's mattress over so that if the soldiers come searching, they won't feel his body heat on the bed.

Next she tries to stand on the edge of the bottom bunk to reach up and turn the Canadian's mattress. She is short and so pregnant, her belly gets in the way. I suck in my breath as she almost falls backwards. She tries to flip over the long heavy kapok mattress on the top bunk. Again she tries.

Soldiers' yells come from the far end of the building. Did the ooms get to the woods safely? Will the Nazis barge in before Tante has hidden all the evidence? Will they look in the manure pile? No, they're looking for somebody, not something.

I want to crawl out of hiding to help Tante. She's still clinging with one hand to the edge of the top bunk, trying to flip the mattress over with the other. My hand, my arm, my whole body moves every time

Tante makes a move. But I dare not leave the cupboard. I'm not like Tante and Oom.

Finally, I sigh with relief. Tante has turned the mattress over. She pulls the corners into place and steps down. I want to run and hug her, my brave tante.

I listen for noises outside. I hear soldiers marching, left, right, left, right. Then I realize the noise is my own heart beating. The yelling has stopped and all is nighttime still again with only the bombers flying over, high, high above us.

I wish I was like the other children, fast asleep, warm and snug under the extra blankets from the ooms. Sometimes it's easier not to know everything.

CHAPTER 4
UNDERGROUND
HIDEOUT

In the morning I like to sleep late, but Tante Mies always gets everyone up right after the neighbor's rooster crows. We are all ready for breakfast. Oom and the Canadian have not come back. Are they safe or did the Nazis find them?

I can't ask because Tante doesn't talk about dangerous secrets. She doesn't even know that I saw what happened last night. I want to find Oom and the Canadian and take them their warm clothes. It's damp and foggy outside. But I have to help set the table instead.

This morning we have broodpap, made of bread, milk and water cooked together. We get this kind of porridge when there's not very much bread or milk left. Sometimes we eat the porridge with sweet sugar-beet stroop, other times with butter.

Today the stroop is all gone and the milkman hasn't come yet. But I won't complain that the broodpap is only watery milk with gooey little gray pieces floating around in it. In Rotterdam my friends have even less to eat.

Tante Mies serves everyone a big ladleful. "Eet smakelijk," she says.

I'm just about to put the first spoonful in my mouth when Wiese jumps up. "The milkman, the milkman!" she calls.

The milkman has lots of butter today, so Tante Mies asks for two pounds. She hands him two pails so he can fill them with milk.

"Your milk is getting more blue every day," Tante says.

The milkman shrugs. "If you'd rather not buy it, others will."

Tante looks unhappy, but she takes the two pails of milk anyway. We all know that it's blue because the milkman adds water to it before he sells it.

Tante gets two bottles of yogurt and a chunk of cheese as well. Oom Frans probably gave her extra coupons. It's part of his resistance job to get food ration cards and coupons illegally and give them to people who hide others.

"It's my turn," Wiese calls when Tante is finished buying things.

Four-year-old Wiese and Marjan and Rita, who are both three, take turns sitting up on the milkman's wagon for a ride. They get to hold the horse's reins. Us older kids — thirteen-year-old Peter, twelve-year-old Reinder and I — take turns walking beside the horse.

Rita whines that she wants a turn on the wagon, but

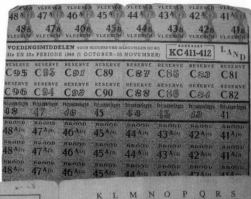

The Nazis wanted to control who bought food and how much they were getting. So they made up a system where everyone needed to have a "stam kaart," or ration card (above), to collect coupons to buy food. Jews and other people in hiding could not use their own cards to get coupons. So members of the Dutch Resistance stole coupons as well as blank ration cards and used them to buy extra food. There were coupons for meat, snacks and bread (top) and for heating and cooking fuel (left).

she had a ride yesterday. Tante Toos comes outside. "Come, lieveling," she says, "You can help me put a little piece of butter in everyone's broodpap."

When the wagon reaches the neighbor's house, Wiese hands the reins back to the milkman and climbs down. We run home. I'm especially hungry knowing that the broodpap will have melted butter in it.

After we finish eating, Tante Mies stands up and says that she hopes the food will do us good. That's the sign for everyone to check the list of jobs she has put up.

Everyone who stays here, even for a short while, has to take turns doing different tasks like boiling water and doing the dishes, cleaning the floors with a broom and a wet rag, cleaning the tables and chairs, the counters, windows, stove. There is always so much to clean. Then there's the laundry and the ironing and the mending and darning socks and knitting and sewing and cutting wood and chopping and stacking and... The list is too long.

Every week the list rotates, and today I have to help look after the outside fire. Mrs. Reyne and Mrs. Laroy are making beet stroop. First they cut the big white beets into strips and then cook them over the fire. Peter, Reinder and I have to stoke the fire and bring enough wood over to keep it burning all morning.

We take one-hour shifts, stoking and stacking the wood. It's hard work. The flames need to be just right so that the heavy beets slowly turn into syrup without burning. Mrs. Laroy and Mrs. Reyne can't stop stirring or the beets will turn into a horrible mess. And then

Reinder pursuing
his favorite
pastime.

we'd have nothing sweet to eat at all because there's no sugar. The Nazis took it all.

Beet stroop is very sticky. If you drop a little bit on the floor and step on it in stocking feet, you're stuck. Maybe tomorrow we'll have broodpap with stroop instead of butter. Maybe we'll even have a slice of bread with butter and stroop later today. With a glass of milk. If we do, it'll almost be like there's no war going on.

Tante Mies and Tante Toos are doing the laundry. They heat full kettles on the stove and then pour the hot water into a tub outside. Tante Toos beats the long-handled soap holder in the water until bubbles appear. Then she scrubs the clothes, sheets, diapers and towels on a board. Tante Mies rinses the laundry in a tub of clean water and wrings it out. Every few minutes she stops and looks around. She doesn't usually need to rest so much. What is she doing?

She carries a basket of wet clean clothes to the line that stretches across the yard and begins to hang them up. But she's not concentrating on what she's doing and drops a clothes peg. Then she drops a diaper. Marjan hands things back to her.

Tante waddles over to the far end of the clothesline, scanning the trees in the distance. Has she noticed someone lurking in the woods? Have Nazis come to spy on us?

Suddenly I know what she's doing. She's making sure that it's safe for the ooms to come back. I watch her closely for a signal. Tante starts to hum a tune I don't recognize. Then she sings something about sunshine and the fog lifting.

Oom Frans and the Canadian appear at the edge of the trees. I'm so relieved that they're safe! I'm even glad to see the Canadian. Oom and Tante give each other a hug and talk softly. Oom says they're lucky the Nazis didn't search the house this time. He takes a look inside the shed before following the Canadian into the house.

That's when I remember. They couldn't flee to the shed last night when the Nazis were here. There's a hiding place in the shed — there has to be. Oom just went in to check on it!

I finish my shift hauling wood and sit down for a rest. When no one is looking, I saunter into the shed. A mess greets me — shovels, picks, hammers, nails and saws all thrown everywhere. There's never a mess in here. Oom Frans likes his tools to be organized. The Nazis did this.

I scan the cluttered workbench, but except for the mess there's nothing unusual. The walls show no signs of a hiding place, nor do the cupboards, nor the corner where the old wheelbarrow usually stands. I look at the floor. No freshly dug earth. I crawl under the table. Nothing.

I'm about to give up when I take one last look at the far wall under the table. A tiny scrap of blue cloth has caught on one of the boards. It's from Peter's shirt — I'm sure of it. This morning Tante Toos scolded him for being so careless and getting a rip in his sleeve. New clothes are hard to find. One of the men who stayed at Het Buitenhuis for a few days gave Peter the blue shirt only last week.

I pick the scrap of cloth off and push at the board. The rough wood moves slightly. I push harder and notice that a small square section of wall is loose. When I press both hands against it, a trapdoor swings out of the wall into the space behind it.

If Peter went through this opening, then so can I.

Careful not to get my clothes caught, I crawl into a dark underground hideout. I don't have a flashlight, but by the dim light that comes through the trapdoor I count six iron cots with blankets. Beside me stands a barrel. I lift the lid and see water with a ladle. Another barrel holds dry biscuits. The hideout is cramped, dark and musty smelling. The dirt walls feel damp.

People hide here when the Nazis come. They can even sleep here and have something to eat. A shiver runs through my whole body. I crawl back out, closing the trapdoor carefully behind me.

Outside the fog has thickened and it feels like we're

in a lost world. Clumps of trees look like ghostly guards. Sounds are muffled.

War is like fog. Everything is dull, cold, gray and secret. You never know when someone might sneak up, when something... I suck in my breath. One of the trees in front of me moved. I take a step back and look harder. Then I slowly let my breath escape.

It is just Oom Frans in his long dark coat, staring off into the distance.

CHAPTER 5
PETER OPPENHEIMER

I'm glad that Peter and I have to work together stacking firewood for the winter. We load pieces of wood into the wheelbarrow and push it to the shed. I watch Peter to see if he looks at the trapdoor. He doesn't. He doesn't look around at all. He just unloads the wood.

After stacking the logs in a neat pile, we walk back to where the men are cutting up trees, one man at each end of the big saw.

"How did you rip your sleeve?" I ask Peter.

He shrugs. Peter doesn't talk much. Not like Reinder, who can yap my ear off. Peter has a slight German accent. I wonder if he worries about saying some words differently, like the Nazis. We walk back in silence while I mull over what Reinder has told me about Peter.

After Peter came from Germany he stayed with Reinder's family in Rotterdam. How he got there I

**Oom Frans
with Reinder
and Peter.**

don't know, but he was starving and the van Tyens fed
him until he was healthy again. A few months ago the
van Tyens themselves started running out of food, so
they sent Reinder and Peter to stay here at Het
Buitenhuis. The van Tyens and the Braals are good
friends.

{37}

After the Nazis controlled Holland they began to persecute Dutch Jews. They forced them to wear yellow stars bearing the word "Jood." They forbade them to go to schools, stores, parks, theaters and other public places. Many Jews were arrested and sent to labor camps or concentration camps such as Theresienstadt, Auschwitz, Dachau or Bergen-Belsen. Some managed to avoid arrest by going into hiding. Most people who were sent to camps were killed or became so ill and weak from maltreatment and starvation that they died before the war was over.

After we load the wheelbarrow again, we walk back to the shed. "Why did you leave Germany?" I ask.

Peter's eyes almost jump out of his face. "Who told you?" he whispers.

I shrug my shoulders as if it's not a big deal.

"We were hungry," he says. "I have to get this sliver out of my hand." He walks away.

Now I'm more curious than ever. I unload the wood and wait until he comes back. The big wheelbarrow is too hard for one of us to balance. We each have to take a handle.

As we push the wheelbarrow back across the lawn I try to get more answers. I know I'm not supposed to ask questions, but I can't stop myself.

"You said 'we were hungry.' Where is your father?"

"In Theresienstadt."

I breathe in sharply. Theresienstadt is a camp. "You're a Jew!"

He glances at me and then quickly turns away.

"I won't tell," I whisper fiercely. "You're my friend. They'd never get that information out of me. Never!"

Peter looks grateful. I feel badly for making him scared, so I say, "My parents are in hiding too."

"They left you behind?" Peter asks.

I nod before I press on, wanting to know all there is to know. "Who else is in your family?"

"My mother and brother."

"Where are they now?"

"I don't know. My brother was sent to another family when I went to the van Tyens. My mother went to England."

We load up with wood and walk back the other way. My hand hurts. I think I have a new blister. Finally, I ask, "Why didn't your mother take you?"

Peter shoves the wheelbarrow hard, almost tipping it over. "We were in the port of Hoek van Holland, on the wharf about to board a ship to England. The war had just started and important Dutch government people were going on the ship too. There was a huge crowd and everyone was pushing and yelling.

"My mother was carrying two suitcases, so she

couldn't hold onto us. We were supposed to show our papers, but the crowd pushed her up the gangplank. We couldn't get to her. She cried and tried to get back down. But everyone kept yelling and shoving. My brother was holding my hand. He fell down, then I fell too. People stepped on us. They trampled over us. Everybody was scared and in a hurry. We didn't make it onto the ship.

"A man saw us at the wharf. We were hurt and crying. He took me to Mr. van Tyen's house. My brother went somewhere else. The man promised we wouldn't be separated for long, but that was more than four years ago."

We sit on the stack of firewood, Peter's eyes swimming in tears. I don't know what to say. I think about Mama and Papa.

"You'll find everybody again," I finally mumble. "Your mother is safe in England. Your father will get out of the camp and send for all of you when the war is over. It'll be over soon. Everybody says so. France and Belgium are already free. Parts of Holland too. The Allied soldiers are working together to beat the Nazis."

We continue our trips with the wheelbarrow. The woodpile grows and the fog lifts.

"You were in the secret hideaway," I say when we reach the shed again.

"How do you know?"

"I saw a piece of your shirt stuck to the trapdoor."

"Don't tell anyone," he begs.

"Of course not. You're my friend. Does Reinder know?"

Peter shakes his head. "I don't think so." He frowns. "If he did, he would have told already."

"I can keep a secret," I say.

CHAPTER 6
HELPING

Oom Frans asks Peter, Reinder and me to clean up the mess the soldiers made in the shed. Peter and I look at each other and then at the wall where the trapdoor is hidden. We say nothing. We put the old wheelbarrow back in its corner and tidy the workbench.

Oom Frans looks pleased when he comes to inspect our job. "Good work," he praises. "The baker's here. Now, go and help Tante bring in the bread."

That means there is lots of extra bread and Oom will take some of it on his bicycle to Rotterdam. He'll ride through the town of Oostvoorne, across the guarded bridge over the wide Maas River, along the quiet side roads and into the city.

Oom's bicycle has homemade tires. Because of the war, no one can buy bicycle tires anymore. So people ride on bare rims, or they make tires from rubber or wood. When you ride on Oom's bike everything in your body rattles.

Oom Frans often organized sports activities such as this game of tug-of-war to help keep everyone in shape.

I wonder if Papa and Mama have bread to eat. When I lived in the city with my parents, Oom Frans often came to our house. He even stayed overnight sometimes. I didn't know his name then. He was simply the man with the black beard.

Oom Frans shakes my shoulder. "You dreamer," he says, smiling. "Go on and help Peter and Reinder bring in the last loaves."

The baker rides from door to door selling the bread. I notice that the big woven basket hanging from his handlebars is almost empty. He loads two big loaves of roggebrood and three loaves of brown bread on my outstretched arms.

"That should do it," he says. "I'll see you tomorrow."

He takes several brown loaves from the packs on the

back of his bike and stacks them in the basket before he closes the lid. There is no white bread. We haven't been able to buy white bread or buns for at least a year.

Inside the house the four women are already slicing the bread. "Oh good, roggebrood," Tante Toos says, eyeing the heavy dark loaves in my arms.

"We'll keep a loaf of roggebrood," Tante Mies says. "There's a small chunk of cheese left. Along with the butter it'll be a treat."

"Roggebrood with butter and cheese, and brown bread with stroop." Tante Toos's eyes light up as she starts to butter a tall stack of slices.

"We need two hundred sandwiches," Tante Mies says.

That means Oom Frans will visit many people. He won't be back for hours, probably not until tomorrow. Today is a good day to travel because it's foggy. He'll have the sandwiches hidden in secret pockets Tante has sewn into his clothes, and into other places like his bicycle bags and bicycle muffs.

Oom Frans is lucky that the government pays his wages as an employee of the water board. They know that he hardly has time to work at his job nowadays, he's so busy in the resistance. But his wages keep coming anyway, and Oom and Tante use the money for food and clothes for everybody. We are all lucky.

The next morning Oom still hasn't returned home. I have the chore of cleaning the common-room tables and chairs. Tante always wants everything to be spotless, even though there's a war going on.

I swirl a rag through a pail of cold water, making a

trail in the soap bubbles. Tante and the Canadian are talking and laughing as they do the dishes. Tante is teaching him more Dutch words.

"Open the door for some fresh air," Tante says to me. "It's such a beautiful day."

I shake the soap bubbles off my hands, open the door and look out. Everyone else has left to help get a big load of wood from the back of the property. I wish I was running around outside with the others. I sigh, swirl the rag in the water, wring it out and wipe some of the chairs.

Suddenly I hear, "Guten Morgen." I freeze, my hands squeezing the rag. There's a Nazi at the door.

I stare at the Canadian. His face is white, his eyes big as he slowly backs out of the room into one of the dorms.

I want to jump up and run out with the Canadian, but I can't move. The Nazi will know that we are in hiding. If I stop looking at him and turn away, he will shoot me. He will shoot Tante because she is hiding the Canadian.

Slowly, Tante dries her hands on the kitchen towel. She waddles to the door, sticking her belly out even more than usual. "Can I help you?" she asks.

The Nazi's blue eyes roam from the common room to Tante's face to the doors leading to the dorms. He's not much taller than Tante, and now I notice that he is not carrying a gun. He says something in German.

"Pardon," Tante answers in Dutch.

I know Tante can speak German very well. She's trying to give the Canadian time to get out the back door, warn the others and hide.

The Nazi speaks slowly in German. Even I can understand this time. He points to the red cross on his arm band and says he's a doctor. He's looking for the building that has forty beds. He wants to use it as a hospital for his soldiers.

Forty beds! He means Het Buitenhuis. He's taking our home away from us. We'll be put in a camp.

Tante looks right at the Nazi and shakes her head. "Sir," she says, in Dutch. "I have lived here all my life and I have never heard of such a place."

I hold my breath. The Nazi knows Tante is not telling the truth. He knows it just as surely as I know it. I see it in his face.

His eyes take in the common room again. He glances at me. He looks at the door the Canadian disappeared through. Then he stares hard at Tante. She stares back at him.

Finally, the Nazi says, "Don't worry, ma'am. I will never bother you again." He turns and walks away.

I let out my breath slowly.

Tante looks at me. "Don't be afraid," she says in a shaky voice. "He won't be back. There are good Nazis too."

CHAPTER 7
DANGER

Oom Frans has been to the city several more times. This morning he brought home three people whose names I don't know. One man is so thin, he has to hold up his pants with a piece of string. He has bare feet, his cheeks have caved in, and his eyes seem dead. He doesn't look at anybody, he doesn't talk, and he doesn't help with any chores. He just sits in a corner of the common room. I'm scared of him.

On his way home from Rotterdam, Oom Frans stopped at some of the farms nearby. He collected one whole bicycle bag full of potatoes and sugar beets, and the other bag full of cabbages, carrots, turnips, apples and pears.

We each have a thick slice of bread and cheese, a glass of milk and an apple. I haven't felt this full for weeks. Some days Tante Mies can only give us one thin slice of bread with a bit of jam, tomato or cucumber on it. Then she gathers all the bread crumbs and divides them among us. But we don't complain. We're not allowed to talk about food or how hungry we are. "It doesn't help," Tante says.

The fall weather is still nice, so the adults take chairs outside. They sit back for a rest, some even taking off their warm sweaters so they can soak up the last bit of sunshine.

Tante Toos spreads a blanket on the grass and starts reading the story of "Little Thumb" to the younger children. Reinder is outside too, practicing his part for the play.

Dressing up and acting out favorite fairy tales helped keep the children at Het Buitenhuis amused.

Oom Frans and Tante Mies put on sprookjes plays sometimes. We've done *Sleeping Beauty*, *Puss in Boots*, *Snow White* and *Hansel and Gretel*. I got to be the cat in *Puss in Boots* last week. Reinder is going to be the wolf in *Little Red Riding Hood*. The plays are a lot of fun — even the adults enjoy them.

As I am looking through the bookshelf to find something to read, the new man with the dead eyes gets up and walks into the kitchen. When he thinks nobody is watching, he grabs a big raw potato and eats it — skin, dirt and all. I turn away and go outside.

Suddenly I hear grunting in the ditch nearby. The neighbor's fat pig is rooting in the mud.

"Shoo," I yell, waving my arms. "Shoo, get home."

The pig snorts. I pick up a stick and wave it near his big dirty head. "Shoo," I yell again. The pig squeals and runs off.

I'm glad the neighbor didn't come looking for his pig. He might have seen us all out here in the sun. We don't know if he can be trusted with our secrets. He has a secret of his own though — the pig. The Nazis don't know he has it. No one's allowed to keep pigs without a Nazi permit.

I'd like to catch the porker for ourselves. We almost never have meat. Two weeks ago Tante bought a little piece of pork for a lot of money. But it was a funny color, and it smelled bad. Dr. Monster was here that morning, so Tante Mies asked him if he thought we could still eat it. The doctor smelled the pork and said yes, he thought so. We all had a small piece that day with real gravy on our potatoes.

I wander closer to two of the new men so that I can eavesdrop. They are talking about how Oom Frans gets food from the farmers. He tells them that if they don't sell or give him food, he will report them to the Dutch government after the war.

"Did you see how he stared at them with those fiery eyes?" one of the men says.

"Everyone knows the war will be over soon," the other one replies. "Even so, Frans should be careful. The NSB is everywhere."

Peter waves at me then looks at the long poles leaning against the shed wall.

"Sure," I nod, knowing what he's thinking. We take off our sweaters and shoes and grab the poles so that we can vault over the ditch.

"Who's that?" Peter says suddenly.

Someone is racing toward Het Buitenhuis on a bicycle. He's pedaling so hard, he's almost bent double into the wind.

I drop my pole. "A man in a uniform. Come on."

We run over to tell Oom, who scrambles up from the grass.

"It's Mr. de Kruif," he says, just as Oostvoorne's policeman jumps off his bike.

"Ten minutes," he gasps, breathing so hard he can barely get the words out. "Someone's coming to search for people in hiding." Mr. de Kruif leans heavily on his bike. "I had to give him directions. I gave him the

**Two of the older
children take a turn
at pole jumping.**

long way around the woods. You have ten minutes!"

Oom is already motioning for everyone to take their chairs back into Het Buitenhuis. "Who is it?" he asks Mr. de Kruif.

"Someone from the NSB who works for the Ortskommandant. He has permission to search your place. Hurry!" he says, jumping back on his bicycle.

Tante Mies waddles inside. She's so pregnant now, she can't hurry.

Oom calls all of us together. "Wiese," he directs his oldest daughter, "take the book and read to the little ones."

Wiese looks frightened. "I can't read this…"

"Pretend," Oom says calmly. "Here, sit on the blanket. You know the story of Little Thumb and how brave he was even though he was so small."

Baby Frank starts to cry. Wiese, her eyes big, holds her brother close and opens the book. Marjan snuggles next to her to see the pictures.

Oom pats Wiese's head. "That's a good girl," he smiles. "You're brave too."

He turns, the smile gone. "Everyone to the woods. Follow me."

We hurry after Oom as he leads us to a ditch running through a thick clump of trees. "In there," he points.

The ditch isn't very big, but we all get in and cover ourselves with leaves.

"Not a sound," Oom says.

We don't need to be told. We sit side by side. No one moves. I strain to hear noises coming from the house but hear nothing.

When we first sat down, Peter grabbed my hand. Now he squeezes my fingers so hard I'm sure they will be bruised, maybe even broken. A fly starts buzzing somewhere in the leaves close to my ear.

When I don't think I can last another minute, I hear other noises. A twig snaps. Footsteps rustle in the leaves nearby.

We've been found! We'll all be taken prisoner. Or we'll be shot, Oom and Tante included. Only the little kids will be left sitting on the blanket, Wiese forever reading about the mean ogre.

Some of the younger children play in a dry ditch on the grounds of Het Buitenhuis.

"No!" I want to yell. I press my lips shut. "Not a sound, not a sound, not a sound," my head hammers.

"Come on out!"

It's Oom's voice.

Someone rustles beside me. "Frans is alone," says one of the men who arrived last night. "We're safe."

Suddenly, for no reason at all, I notice that he has an accent. Maybe he's a German Jew, or he's French, or English. Why do I even care? We're safe!

I'm one of the last to get up, to give my squashed hand a chance to stop throbbing. But I don't tell Peter how much it hurts.

"He's gone," Oom tells us. "Mies managed to hide

everything in time. He had the gall to say he was disappointed that he didn't find anyone to report to the Nazis."

"That stinking piece of filth," one of the men says. "Will he be back?"

"I hope not, but we need to be more careful," Oom says, running his hands through his hair. "No one in hiding can wander around on the driveway or in the direction of the neighbors anymore. None of you is to be seen, understand?" He looks at us sternly.

We slowly walk out of the clump of trees. The weak autumn sun has been replaced by thick gray rain clouds.

CHAPTER 8
SINTERKLAAS EVE, DECEMBER 5

Almost a month ago Jannie Torreman came to Het Buitenhuis. She is not in hiding. She's a midwife helping Tante Mies.

Tante and Oom have a new baby, a little girl, Els. The day she was born we celebrated by drinking hot milk and eating rusks with chocolate sprinkles, which Tante had saved especially for the occasion.

We all get to take turns holding the baby. She is so cute, with tiny little wriggly toes, and fingers that grab onto your finger and won't let go.

The days are short and the misty rains keep the gray dawn hanging around until early dusk takes its place. We need some fresh air, so even though it's wet we go out and dance the Zevensprong, jumping around the puddles to get all seven of the dance steps in before we get soaked. Oom Frans laughs loudly when a fat raindrop splats on his nose.

The sky turns darker. We rush indoors just as the

The baby at bath time. The large tub was also used for laundry, for rinsing fruit and vegetables, and for storing water when the power was off.

wind starts to howl and the clouds burst overhead.

Darkness glides in. The adults blacken the windows with paper, securely pushing the edges into each corner. No one will be able to look in from the outside, not even the men from the blackout patrol who come to inspect that no light escapes.

Every night, and often during the day as well, the Nazis cut off all the electricity on the island. Sometimes one of Oom Frans's friends secretly turns the power back on so we can use the pump to get water.

Right now though, we don't mind the dark. We have a light of our own. Oom brings in Tante Mies's bicycle and sets it upside-down in the common room.

He pushes the dynamo's round top against the bike's front wheel. He asks me to turn one of the pedals round and round. When I push the pedal, the wheel turns the dynamo and it powers the lamp. Oom bends the lamp so that a circle of light falls on the long table.

Everyone sits around the table with pots of potatoes and kale to get ready for tomorrow's stamppot. The paring knives cut and scrape softly while Tante Toos reads a story.

Tante Mies breastfeeds Els. When the baby finishes, Jannie changes her cloth diaper and puts her in her crib. Mrs. Reyne takes her new baby, Brenda, over to Tante Mies. Mrs. Reyne has no milk to give, so Tante Mies breastfeeds Brenda as well.

The dynamo whirrs and the rain taps on the windows. Together we listen and work, safe within this circle of light.

Afterwards Jannie plays her guitar and sings a lullaby. Oom Frans joins in, singing harmony. He used to sing harmony with Mama while Papa played the piano. That night I dream of Papa, Mama, Oom and Tante singing and dancing around a fat moon.

•

The adults have been whispering and grinning and writing words on scraps of paper all week. The common

When there was no electricity the Braals improvised using a bicycle generator and light.

room is tidy, the fire crackling, the kettle humming on top of the stove. The two littlest babies are asleep in their cribs, but even the toddlers get to stay up late because it's Sinterklaas Eve.

Tante Toos opens the lid on the piano and Jannie picks up her guitar. Soon we are all singing the special Sinterklaas songs. Between songs our ears are tuned for sounds. Not for sounds of Nazis coming, but for sounds of Sinterklaas knocking on the door, of his helper, Piet, climbing on the roof.

The door opens a crack and suddenly the room is full of treats. We all dive under the chairs and tables, gathering as many sweets as we can. This year they are not the usual pepernoten. Instead they are pieces of broken candy. Never mind. I'm too excited to care.

When all the sweets have been piled on the table, the door creaks and Piet's face peeks in. His eyes scan the room. We sing the Sinterklaas song again, our bodies bursting with energy.

Sinterklaas walks in, his big book under his arm. Even though there is a war going on, Sinterklaas has come to visit us.

At first little Frank cries, but Tante Mies rocks him on her knee and whispers in his ear.

Sinterklaas sits down on the best chair. I notice that he is wearing Pieter Langendoen's boots. He opens his book and calls Reinder forward. "Reinder, you have been such a hardworking student," he says. "Piet tells me you like to read a lot. Is that true?"

Reinder nods.

Mies loved to take pictures of her family like this one showing Frans playing with their baby.

"Piet, I think you may have something for him," Sinterklaas says.

Piet opens his gunny sack and hands Reinder a book. Reinder beams.

Next Sinterklaas calls Marjan up. Oom Frans has to go with her because Marjan is afraid to go by herself. She sits on Sinterklaas's knee and Piet gives her a little dress for her cloth doll, since she has been such a good helper to Tante Mies.

Peter's turn comes next. I'm surprised that he looks almost as shy as Marjan. He stares at the floor, but he's happy when Piet gives him a new hat.

Finally, it's my turn. Sinterklaas says he's proud of me for helping to stack so much firewood. And for cleaning up the shed, even when I had a big blister on my hand. Piet reaches into the gunny sack and brings out a pair of beautiful red mittens.

"Thank you, Sinterklaas!" I try on the thick wool mittens. They fit perfectly. Now my hands will stay warm. They will no longer be chapped and painful from the cold.

After Sinterklaas leaves, Tante Mies helps us divide the candy into equal piles for all the children. The adults have made little presents with poems for everybody. One after another we read the poems out loud. Most of them are very silly. Sometimes the adults laugh so hard they have to wipe tears from their eyes.

When all the poems have been read and all the presents opened, we sing the thank-you song. We keep singing until the littlest children are asleep. Finally, I stumble off to bed and fall asleep too, my new mittens still on my hands.

CHAPTER 9
FALSE LIVES

A few days later, when I'm reading on my bed, I hear voices coming from one of the little bedrooms at the end of the dorm. I sneak closer and recognize Jannie's giggle. Then I hear the Canadian talking about how he came here. He speaks Dutch so well now, I can understand everything he says. Sometimes he uses English words too, and then Jannie answers in English.

The Canadian has hepatitis, so he needs to stay in bed. Dr. Monster told him to eat lots of fruits and vegetables and candies to get over the jaundice. The Canadian lets us kids take a candy from his big jar if we stare at him hard enough. Oom and Tante don't know that we go to him to get sweets.

He starts telling Jannie about his family. They think he is missing in action and presumed dead. He wants to get in touch with them and tell them he is alive. But he isn't allowed because the message could be intercepted by the Nazis and put resistance members in danger.

He tells Jannie that sometimes he feels depressed. Most of the crew of his plane died when they crashed. Oom found out that their captain and pilot, Jock Reilly, is the only other one who survived. He was taken prisoner by the Nazis. The Canadian wishes he could see Jock Reilly again. And he wants to get back to his RAF base in England. But he can't. All he can do is wait.

Then he starts to talk about Canada and my ears perk up. It sounds exciting. I'm going to find books to read about Canada.

Now there's silence. I quickly back away from the door. The Canadian and Jannie! A grin spreads across my face as I leave the dorm. If Jannie likes the Canadian a lot, he must be okay.

That evening when I'm supposed to be in bed I crawl back into the hiding cupboard. I see Tante Mies

poking at the wet wood in the stove. She coughs when a big cloud of smoke belches right into her face and she closes the stove quickly.

Heavy old irons, from before the days of electricity, came into use once again during the war.

Mrs. Laroy is ironing with both of Tante's flatirons. She uses one iron while the other sits on the stove to get hot. She puts her fingers in a cup of water, sprinkles drops on her best dress and presses the hot flatiron down. The dress steams. It looks nice enough to wear to a film, but we can't go anywhere.

Oom Frans is working on false identity cards. He is

The Nazis could stop anyone at anytime and ask to see their identity card, like this one belonging to Frans Braal. Resistance workers stole blank ID cards so that they could make up false cards for people who needed to hide their real identities. A false ID card with a new photo and fingerprint gave the bearer a made-up name, place of birth, address and job. With these IDs people could continue to go out into the street and even get food-ration cards and coupons.

good at filling in the cards and signing false signatures so that they look real.

Tante Toos helps stamp the cards. She wants to help because the Nazis captured her husband in a razzia. Soldiers walked into their house without knocking, pointed a gun at Tante Toos's husband and told him they were taking him away to work in the war factories. Tante doesn't know where he is or how he is doing. She says that by stamping the cards she's helping to save other Dutch families from being torn apart.

"Listen," Oom Frans says suddenly.

The adults stop peeling potatoes, their knives in midair. Panic steals across Tante Toos's face. Everyone is silent.

"What is it?" Tante Mies finally whispers.

"Footsteps," Oom says.

No one can look out because the windows are covered with blackout paper. Oom Frans quietly gathers up the ID cards. He slides them under some books on the shelf. The ink pad follows. Tante Toos hands him the stamp. Looking around for a second, he drops the stamp into a barrel of onions in the far corner. He pushes the stamp down deep before he and Tante Toos each grab a knife and start peeling potatoes.

The Canadian takes the men who are here in hiding to the other big dorm. They will slip out the back door if they need to go to the shed.

The rest of the adults peel potatoes quietly, their heads tilted, their ears straining for sounds. There is silence except for the droning of planes far overhead and the occasional plop as a peeled potato is dropped into the big pot of water.

Oom gets up and opens the front door a crack. "Hello?" he calls.

No response.

Oom shrugs. "No one," he says, closing the door and taking another potato.

After a while he washes his hands and calls the men back from the dorm. He pulls the ID cards out from under the books and gives the ink pad to Tante Toos. She looks for the stamp, lifting up an onion here and there. One of the men helps her. They take the top layer of onions out of the barrel. No stamp. They empty the next layer. No stamp.

Jannie starts to laugh. She helps take the next layer of onions out. The table is now full of rolling onions but no stamp.

Two of the men pick up the barrel, turn it over and empty it onto the floor. Onions roll everywhere.

Finally, Jannie sees the stamp with its round onion-colored handle lying under the table.

"Good camouflage," one of the men says. They all laugh as they collect the onions and go back to work.

I leave the cupboard, crawl into bed and go to sleep.

CHAPTER 10
THE LONG
COLD WINTER

Just when I've started thinking that the Canadian is a nice man, he has to leave. The Allied troops are coming closer and the Nazis are getting more desperate. They've increased their searches on the island and have found many people in hiding. Het Buitenhuis is getting too dangerous, so the Canadian and a few others are saying good-bye. They're going into hiding somewhere else. The Canadian says he'll come back to see us when the war is over.

Jannie's going home too. I'll miss them both. They were fun to be around because they laughed a lot.

Two days ago it got very cold, and now Christmas is here. Tante says we won't celebrate the holiday. But we do have rusks with stroop for breakfast and some free time to play games.

Tante found a handful of dried peas to pop. She drops the peas onto the stove top. When they're hot they dance, rolling and jumping back and forth until – *pop!* – they jump off the stove. We find them, divide them equally and eat them. Delicious! We'll also eat many people's favorite food today – two whole Brussels sprouts each with lots of mashed potatoes.

I wonder if Papa and Mama are celebrating Christmas the way we used to, with a tree full of real candles and little chocolate and sugar wreaths. We would sing around the tree, and Papa would read a story. Then we'd eat sugar bread and raisin bread and stollen. And we always had baked rabbit. And we'd go to church to see the manger scene.

I want to go home.

•

This winter feels longer and colder than usual. I can see more wrinkles on Oom and Tante's faces. But with us kids they are happy, sometimes fake happy.

Most of us at Het Buitenhuis have caught hepatitis. The Canadian had it first. Now that he's gone, one after another we've been sick. Oom Frans and Tante Mies are the only ones who haven't got jaundice.

Oom's really funny, trying to cheer us up. He races around the dorms from bed to bed on a tiny bicycle like a clown, his knees sticking up in the air as he rides. He brings us water, and fruit or candy, if he has any. He fluffs up our pillows and tells silly stories.

At least we are warm these days. Oom found out that a load of coal bricks was going to be delivered to some houses that the Nazis had taken from Dutch people. He went over and added his address to the list on the order form, so some of the Nazis' coal was delivered here. Now we have both coal and wood to burn in the stove.

Sometimes Oom takes a small load of wood or coal to people in Rotterdam. Many of them have only tiny emergency stoves in one room of their houses for heat and cooking.

Most of the schools have been closed for a long time. The Nazis have taken over the buildings. Tante Mies teaches us at home when we are not sick or too busy with our jobs. She has two new helpers as well, Oom Frans's sister, Rietje, and Oom's stepsister, Francien. They are both fifteen years old, and they look after the little children.

Tante is teaching me how to read better. I used to feel kind of stupid, especially since I hadn't been to school for so long, but now I can read really fast. I've read every fairy tale in Tante's sprookjes books. I like the ones by Hans Christian Andersen best.

Today I am presenting a project on Princess Juliana. I chose her because she is living in Canada. Ever since I overheard the Canadian talking to Jannie about Canada I've wanted to go there.

I'm wearing Reinder's orange shirt. First I read the part that has a lot of dates and royal names and titles. The adults listen politely, but the little kids start fidgeting. Then I start reading the good parts, and everyone pays attention.

"When the Nazis first invaded our country, in May

Princess Juliana and her children spent the war years in Canada. Prince Bernhard often visited them. Here the royal family poses for a picture soon after the birth of Princess Margriet.

of 1940, Princess Juliana and her family hid in a secret place. After two days in hiding they fled to England. Prince Bernhard, her husband, stayed in London, but Princess Juliana and her little daughters, Beatrix and Irene, went to Canada, where it's safe. Princess Juliana had a baby too, Princess Margriet. She was born in Canada a year ago.

"It gets incredibly cold in Canada, even colder than

it gets here when we have to ride our bicycles in freezing sleet. Some areas are so cold that if you touch a bar on the playground with your tongue, it freezes to the metal."

I can't imagine this myself, and I see everyone else in Het Buitenhuis looking surprised. Peter shivers.

I explain that sometimes there is so much snow, it comes up to the roofs of the houses. The hills are even higher than the church steeple, which is the tallest building in Rotterdam. Canadians slide down these hills on little sleds or on pieces of wood.

Francien's eyes get big. Like me, she thinks that sounds exciting. I have never seen a real hill, only pictures of them.

"Princess Juliana goes skating on a canal in Ottawa," I tell everyone.

"Can we go skating too?" Wiese asks.

"Not this winter," Tante says.

I'm glad. My skates are too small to fit under my boots, and the tops of my feet always hurt from the straps being tied so tightly. I can't skate very well, but I miss the street organ that used to play by the frozen lake in Rotterdam, and the hot chocolate and sausage tent. And running around with my friends.

I wonder if anyone is skating in Rotterdam today. We had snow last night and Oom says it was -19°C. The canals will be frozen. I bet the resistance workers are skating from canal to canal rather than riding their bicycles on slippery streets.

Tante asks if my presentation is finished and everyone claps. Francien and Reinder want to see the map I held up.

"Look how huge Canada is compared to tiny little Holland," I say, flipping to a page in the atlas that shows the whole world.

Francien traces the borders of Canada with her finger, a faraway look on her face. She no longer seems as sad as she was yesterday when she got a letter from her mother in Rotterdam. Her mother said she doesn't know how she will continue to feed the family because they have no more bread coupons. She's happy that her daughter is getting fattened up a bit and is learning a lot at the Braals. She wrote that she misses her "sock darner." Francien laughed at that. She wishes she could be home with her family.

We go outside for the afternoon to play in the snow. Peter, Francien and I take turns walking around in Oom Frans's wooden shoes. The snow is just right for sticking to the bottoms, and in no time at all we have tall snow stilts.

The ooms and the other kids make a huge snowman. Next everyone builds a snow wall and pelts it with snowballs. Then we chase Oom Frans who looks like a Canadian polar bear with his beard all white from hoarfrost.

We go back in, laughing and red-cheeked, with frost clinging to our lashes and hair. The common room smells glorious. Tante Mies has made one of my favorite meals — poffert. The baker didn't have enough bread today, so Tante made dough and put it in a cloth

Oom Frans, Reinder, Wiese and Rietje in the midst of a snowball fight. The winter of 1944–45 was unusually cold.

sack to cook in a pot on the stove all afternoon. Now she's cutting a thick slice for each of us. We eat it with melted butter and warm stroop.

The adults will play charades tonight, but I won't be

spying from the cupboard. Nowadays I fall asleep right away in my bed. I pull the sheet and blankets up over my nose because it's so cold. My bed is my warm cozy nest, and if I put my pillow over my head, the planes no longer wake me up.

CHAPTER 11
THE HUNGRY CHILDREN

Today I counted twenty-six people at the table, thirteen of them children. We're busy all the time, cleaning, making meals and stacking as much firewood as we can between rain or snowstorms.

The wind howls like a pack of starving Canadian wolves. When we open the front door, squalls of wetness rush in. They sometimes blow the laundry right off the rack.

I overhear Oom telling Tante that there's no heat in the houses in Rotterdam. The Nazis have cut off all the power and have taken all the coal and other fuel for burning. People are freezing. There are no trees left in the city because they've already been cut down for firewood. People burn their own furniture, cupboards, even every second step of their wooden stairs. They sneak into houses that stand empty to look for doors, window frames, stairs, anything made of wood.

Oom says there's very little food to be found. Some

of the people selling food don't want ration coupons or money anymore. They will only trade — a few carrots for a gold locket or some potatoes for a silver bracelet.

Tante seems so sad I can hardly look at her face. "Bring whoever you must," she says to Oom. "The Nazis can only kill us once. We may as well take in as many as we can."

Oom nods. "The children, especially," he says. "They go around in rags, sometimes even without shoes and socks. They're out on the streets looking for half-rotten food in garbage cans. Or they leave the city with a bicycle, a cart or a baby buggy and walk around the countryside for hours, looking for a farmer who will give them something to eat. They even eat grass or dandelions. They are so hungry, they collapse sometimes."

I leave my hiding place through the little door into the dormitory. I don't want to cry, but tears start to run down my face. I lie down on my bed, my face in my pillow, until the hiccupping stops.

•

The next morning, while we're eating a small breakfast of watery porridge, Oom returns from Rotterdam with several new children. He brings one of them close to the warmth of the stove.

"This is Leendert," he says. "He's six. He needs special care."

Leendert looks so thin and sick, he can hardly stand up. His eyes are way too big for his face. Underneath the dirt his skin looks kind of gray-yellow, even though he's just come in from the cold. His hands are wrapped in pieces of gunnysack. I have never seen anybody as starved as Leendert.

Tante Mies calls the rest of the shy children over. "Sit here," she says. "Get warm."

Tante Toos looks at Leendert's head carefully. "He has lice," she says.

The new arrivals sit with their cold feet on the oven lid and their hands warming over the stove. Some of them cry because of the tingling pain as their hands and feet begin to warm up again.

The four women get busy, stoking the stove, adding more coal and warming extra pots of water. They put four chairs in a row, just like they do for all the little kids every Saturday, which is bath day. They bring out the two tubs we use for washing, two washcloths, soap, scissors and a towel.

The women will move each new child along from chair to chair. The first adult will wash them with lots of soap, the second rinse them, the third dry them, the last comb their hair and cut their nails.

The rest of us put on our coats and boots and go outside to play hide-and-seek in the mist. When we go back in, cold, damp and noisy, the new children are washed and dressed in our clothes and pajamas. Leendert's clothes have been burned in the stove. His head is bald.

Yesterday Tante Mies, Reinder and Francien went to different farms and houses in the area. They found families who were willing to take in one more child.

After a few months Leendert was well enough to play with Wiese and the other children.

Now we say goodbye as one after another the children leave to spend the rest of the war with them.

Poor little Leendert will stay with us. He needs to be on a strict diet. He has edema and he has open sores all over his body from scurvy. Dr. Monster has come to put salve on the sores. Tante Toos says that he will help her save Leendert's life.

CHAPTER 12
SPRING 1945

Yesterday we had a great shock. Oom Frans's friend Pieter Langendoen pushed the door open and came in with the wheelbarrow. Oom was lying in it, his eyes rolling, his face in a grimace, his head lolling back and forth.

Tante screamed. We all backed away.

Oom jumped up and said they were just fooling around, trying to get a laugh out of everyone. Tante wasn't laughing.

It's warm outside most days, but yesterday we had a sudden storm with such strong winds I could barely stand up. Everything got covered with slush and big branches broke off the trees.

Today the sun is shining, most of the slush has melted away, and a few spring flowers are in bloom. I can smell the hawthorn.

Flowers are tough. No matter what falls on them, they spring back up and keep growing. A clump of

narcissus are ready to open their buds at any moment.
I think the flowers will be white.

Leendert walks over to me with a book. He's begin-
ning to look much better. He can play again, and his
hair has grown back, but he can't learn anything new.
When I teach him a word he forgets it right away.
Tante thinks that maybe the starvation and trauma
have affected his brain.

Leendert especially likes to look at the pictures of
Ot and Sien in Tante's children's books. I get him to sit
down beside me and repeat the names of the animals
and the objects. Leendert looks at the pictures for a few
minutes. Then he wipes his nose on his sleeve and wan-
ders back inside.

Oom Frans (left) with his friend Pieter Langendoen and two of the children.

By the spring of 1945, the Germans knew they were losing the war and would have to pay reparations. So they agreed to let Canadian, British and American bomber planes drop food parcels at prearranged times and in certain areas of west Holland. During "Operation Manna" Allied airmen dropped 11,000 pounds of food in ten days, saving thousands of Dutch people's lives.

Several noisy ducks fly overhead and land in the swamp. With the four marbles I won off Peter jiggling in my pocket, I wander over to have a look at them.

In Rotterdam I never saw as many different kinds of birds as I do here. The city seems far away. Mama and Papa are far away. Sometimes I can't even remember their faces.

Oom says the war will be over soon. Everyone has said that for months now. Sometimes, in the distance,

I can see planes dropping packages over Rotterdam. Inside them people find dried fruit, dried meat, potato powder, egg powder, sugar, flour, cheese and, best of all, chocolate.

We are lucky here at Het Buitenhuis. Some of the farmers as well as the greengrocer, Dirk van Rij, secretly give Tante Mies extra food, even if they don't have much left over for themselves. They know Tante has a lot of mouths to feed.

The ducks quack noisily again. I creep closer to the swamp. Are they nesting in the reeds? We'll have lots of eggs to eat then. Maybe we'll even have roast duck one day.

Just as I lower myself to my hands and knees, I hear Oom calling my name. He has a funny catch in his voice.

I scurry from my cover, the ducks flying up in surprise. My boots slosh through puddles as I round the trees to the front lawn.

I freeze. Then a cry tears from my throat as I speed right into Mama's arms.

"Finally!" she says, tears filling her eyes. She presses me close and Papa throws his arms around both of us.

"Lieverd!" Mama's voice is shaking. "Oh, lieverd, we missed you so much."

I look from one to the other, my heart beating wildly. Words won't come to my mouth.

"Rotterdam is free," Papa says. "The Nazis are leaving the city."

Oom Frans cheers. He and Papa thump each other on the back. Francien and Rietje scream and throw their arms around each other. Tante Mies and Tante Toos have happy tears in their eyes. Reinder throws his book in the air. Mrs. Reyne and Mrs. Laroy dance around together.

Oom Frans starts to sing in a very loud voice. Everyone claps and sings and runs around like puppies in springtime. Even Peter sings along. Finally, finally, the war is over.

When everyone calms down a little I ask, "Are we going home, Papa?"

"You'll stay here a bit longer," he says. "Rotterdam isn't safe yet. The Nazis need to move out first. People have to rebuild their houses and stores and offices. And there are still many who are hungry."

"Your papa and I will go into the city tomorrow to start cleaning and repairing our house," Mama adds. "It needs a lot of work. After that you'll come home."

The tantes make hot chocolate. We eat strawberries on slices of white bread that Mama brought. We have our treat out on the lawn. We don't need to worry about who sees any of us. No Nazis with guns will come by. The war is over.

Papa and Mama talk about Rotterdam, about the problems people still have, about the clean-up that will take a long time, about the rebuilding that will take years. I can listen to them if I want to. Nobody stops me. Nobody has secrets.

But instead I wander over to the narcissus. The first bud has opened. The flower is white with a heart of orange.

EPILOGUE

The Braal family and all the people described in this book, with the exception of the narrator and the narrator's parents, lived at Het Buitenhuis from late summer of 1944 to the end of the Second World War. All the events concerning them actually took place.

Mies Braal, her daughter Wiese and Francien van der Pol told me what they remembered about their lives sixty years ago. I made up a fictional narrator who could tell the story from a young person's point of view. The narrator is not introduced by name because he/she stands for all children who go through war.

While the Braals and others all across Holland quietly worked against the Nazis' brutal actions, no one kept a record of their brave deeds. The Dutch resistance workers acted secretly because they had no military power. Their weapons were kindness and cunning rather than tanks and guns. Working out in the open would have cost them their freedom, or in many cases their lives. Instead of planning strategies while sitting in comfortable halls and eating hearty meals, they met in their common rooms, their kitchens, their sheds or even while hiding in ditches.

What these conscientious objectors did, however, is as much a part of history as the Nazis' occupation. Frans and Mies Braal, and thousands of others like them, were first of all humanitarians who did not let their own lack of safety stand in their way. They were in as much danger as soldiers on the front line. While the soldiers were ordered to kill and destroy, the Braals tried to protect and rebuild.

In 1957 the Braal family left Holland to live in the United States. In 1969 they immigrated to the West Kootenays in British Columbia, Canada. There they built a cedar house on three hundred acres of land, which they preserved.

Long after the soldiers had put their medals away, some countries finally thanked the Braals for their heroism. President General Dwight D. Eisenhower of the United States and Sir Winston Churchill of Great Britain sent certificates of appreciation. The Dutch government sent a certificate and a bronze cross in 1982. In 1987, more than forty years after the war, the Honourable George Hees, Minister of Veterans Affairs in Canada, was notified of the Braals' bravery. He presented them with a certificate of gratitude for sheltering a Canadian airman. In 1988 the Jewish War Veterans of the Shalom Legion Branch in Vancouver planted fifty trees in Israel in recognition of the Braals' heroism.

Frans Braal died at age eighty-nine in Nelson, British Columbia, on September 28, 2004. Dutch newspapers acknowledged him as a hero and the irreplaceable leader of Oostvoorne's resistance movement during the Second World War. Mies Braal died on April 20, 2007, at age ninety. Six of the Braal children live in the United States, and the youngest lives in Canada.

Peter Oppenheimer did connect with his mother and brother after the war. His father did not survive. Philip

The Braal family arriving in the United States in 1957.

Pochailo lives in Ontario, Canada. Reinder van Tyen and (Tante) Toos Biesheuvel live in the Netherlands. Francien van der Pol immigrated to British Columbia with her husband, Martin van der Pol, and two children. Pieter Langendoen died soon after the war. Policeman de Kruif was arrested shortly after he warned the Braals of the impending search and spent the last few months of the war in prison, but he survived. Further information is not known about Leendert, Jannie Torreman or others mentioned in this book.

Ann Alma
South Slocan

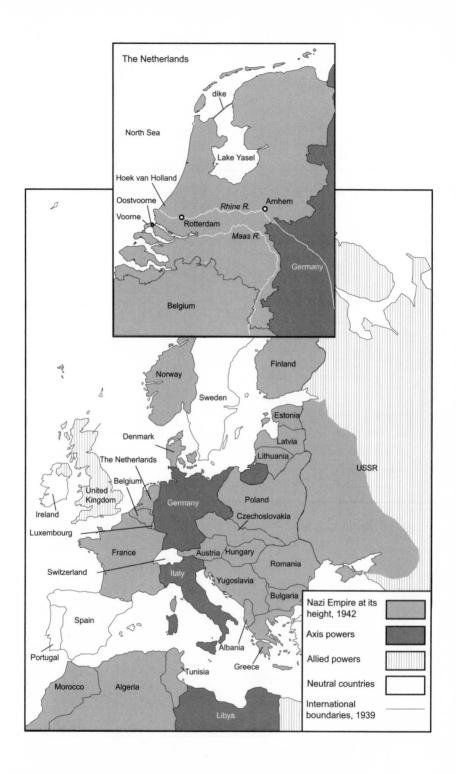

The Netherlands

North Sea

dike

Lake Yasel

Hoek van Holland

Oostvoorne

Voorne

Rhine R.

Arnhem

Rotterdam

Maas R.

Germany

Belgium

Norway

Finland

Sweden

Estonia

Denmark

Latvia

The Netherlands

Lithuania

Belgium

USSR

United Kingdom

Germany

Poland

Ireland

Czechoslovakia

Luxembourg

Austria

Hungary

France

Romania

Switzerland

Italy

Yugoslavia

Bulgaria

Spain

Albania

Greece

Portugal

Tunisia

Morocco

Algeria

Libya

Nazi Empire at its height, 1942

Axis powers

Allied powers

Neutral countries

International boundaries, 1939

HISTORICAL NOTES

The Invasion of the Netherlands

On September 1, 1939, German soldiers under the leadership of Adolf Hitler invaded Poland. Many European countries objected and consequently became involved in a war with Germany and Italy. Soon the Second World War had spread to most parts of Europe and beyond.

The Netherlands, also called Holland, wanted to stay neutral. However, on May 10, 1940, the Nazis suddenly invaded the small country. They needed Holland's many bridges to reach the coast and the North Sea with their tanks and trucks.

Many Dutch people tried to stop the invaders. They blew up some of the bridges and flooded low areas. When the Nazis found that they couldn't move to the coast quickly enough, they bombed Rotterdam. The city burned. Bombs killed and injured many people and destroyed almost 25,000 houses. The Nazis threatened to bomb other cities if the Dutch people didn't cooperate with their armies, and so the government surrendered. A battle between the Nazis and the Dutch would have been like a clash between a tank and a bicycle.

By May 15, 1940, the Nazis occupied all of the Netherlands. The government and the royal family went into exile in England. The Nazis laid claim to many homes, public buildings, meeting halls, schools, even hospitals. If they wanted a building or a plot of land, they gave the owners a notice that said they had to get out. If people didn't leave, the soldiers simply moved the owners and all their possessions out onto the street.

Nazi soldiers took everyone's weapons, cars, and later their radios, telephones, jewelry, and even items such as candlesticks and kettles, which could be melted down to make more weapons.

Dutch Resistance to the War

As the war dragged on from May 1940 into 1944, more and more Dutch people began to rebel against the German occupation of the Netherlands. They were especially shocked by what the Nazis did to Jews and other minorities.

After Hitler came to power, the Nazis persecuted Jews, first in Germany and then in each country they occupied. They tried to round up all Jews, forced them to register and sent them off to work or death camps. Many Jews went into hiding. As the war continued, stories of terrible suffering in the camps reached the people who worked in the resistance movement. During the war most of the Dutch Jewish community – 112,000 people – disappeared into concentration camps. And by the end of the war, six million European Jews had been killed in what is known as the Holocaust.

Dutch men between the ages of sixteen and fifty-five were also in danger of being rounded up in razzias and forced to work in the Nazis' weapons factories. Trucks would block off a section of a city or town. Soldiers would go from door to door ordering all the men into their trucks and then taking them away. Only men who held jobs considered essential such as workers in the food industry, the water board and doctors were left to continue their tasks without the danger of being deported.

Little by little an underground organization, the Dutch Resistance Movement, grew larger and stronger. Its members sabotaged military installations, blew up bridges and railways the Nazis used for troop transport and organized weapon drops from American, British and Canadian planes. They hid or burned registration files to protect people who could be arrested by the Nazis. The resisters hid Jews, other resistance workers and political prisoners. They helped university students who refused to sign the Oath of Allegiance to the Nazis and assisted many other people who were in danger.

Operation Market Garden and the Railway Strike

In September of 1944, in a move called Operation Market Garden, the Allies parachuted troops into the area around the city of Arnhem. Their goal was to capture the most important bridges over the Rhine River. But the troops only managed to hold the bridges for three days before the Nazis recaptured them.

Then the Dutch government, based in London, England, directed the Dutch people to hold a railway strike to stop the Nazis from moving their troops and weapons. All Dutch trains and trams stood empty for the remainder of the war.

But the Nazis took revenge by bringing in their own trains from Germany, and by not allowing any food, clothing or heating fuel to be delivered anywhere. They took away horses, cattle, coal, food stores, many bicycles, wool blankets, watches and anything else they could use. They closed all the waterways and destroyed many boats. The only way the Dutch could move around was on old bicycles with homemade tires, on very old horses and wagons, or on foot.

Dutch Traitors

Not all Dutch people resisted the Nazis. The National Socialist Bond, or the NSB, was a Dutch political party. Many of its members were unhappy with politics in Holland, and they sided with the Nazis once they occupied the country, working as soldiers, chauffeurs, spies and road builders. They double-crossed resistance workers in exchange for pay, extra food, new bicycles, even cars and gasoline from the Nazis.

As the war dragged on they became more and more aggressive. They often led the Nazis to hiding places and helped them in their searches to find Jews and others in hiding. Some members of the NSB even became guards in concentration camps. After the war some of them were hanged and many went to jail.

Liberation

Town by town, field by field, the Canadian troops pushed the Nazis out of the Netherlands. On May 5, 1945, the Nazis surrendered and the Second World War officially ended in Holland. Dutch people welcomed the Canadians like superheroes.

In the fall of 1945 the Dutch people sent 100,000 tulip bulbs to Ottawa, Canada, as a thank-you for keeping their royal family safe and for liberating their country. Princess Juliana, who became Queen Juliana a few years after the war, sent another 20,000 tulip bulbs in 1946. Since then the royal family and the International Flower Bulb Center of Holland have each sent 10,000 bulbs a year. Tulips of all kinds bloom every spring in Canada and Holland – a colorful reminder of friendship and peace.

GLOSSARY

Allies: The countries, including Great Britain, the United
    States, the Soviet Union, Canada, Australia and others,
    that fought against the Axis powers during World War
    II.

Axis: The countries, including Germany, Italy and Japan,
    that fought against the Allies during World War II.

bicycle muff: A padded leather covering strapped to a bicy-
    cle's handlebars in winter to keep the rider's hands
    warm.

bombardier: The member of a bomber plane crew respon-
    sible for aiming and releasing the bombs.

broodpap: Bread porridge.

de Duitsers: The Germans.

dynamo: A generator that could be clipped against the
    front wheel of a bicycle, providing electrical energy as
    the wheel turned to power the bicycle light.

edema: Swelling caused by extra fluids in the body.

eet smakelijk: Eat well.

Gestapo: The German secret police during the Nazi era.

hepatitis: An illness that affects the liver. A person with
    hepatitis may become jaundiced, which means that the
    whites of their eyes and their skin look yellow.

Het Buitenhuis: The house out in the country.

Holocaust: The Nazis' systematic rounding up and killing of
    six million European Jews during the Second World War.

kapok: Silky down from the seeds of the tropical kapok
    tree, used for stuffing pillows and mattresses.

lieveling or lieverd: Darling, love.

Nazis: Members of the National Socialist German

Workers' Party, which came to power in 1933 under
Adolf Hitler's leadership and was defeated in 1945, at
the end of World War II. The racist views of the Nazis
led to the persecution of Jews and the Holocaust.

oom: Uncle.

Ortskommandant: German for regional commander. A
Nazi who controlled a region.

pepernoten: Miniature gingerbread cookies baked to celebrate Sinterklaas Eve on December 5.

RAF: Royal Air Force.

razzia: A raid to round up people to use as slaves.

roggebrood: Heavy black rye bread.

scurvy: A disease caused by a lack of vitamin C. It can
make gums and skin bleed and can keep bones and
teeth from growing properly.

Sinterklaas: A man in a red bishop's mantle and miter
(hat) who rides on a white horse and brings children
presents on December 5. His helper, Piet, listens at
chimneys to find out if the children have been bad or
good.

sprookjes: Fairy tales.

stam kaart: Ration card.

stamppot: Potatoes and one vegetable (such as carrots,
kale, cabbage or turnips) mashed together, usually
served with Dutch sausage.

stollen: Fruit bread with an almond-spice center.

stroop: Syrup.

tante: Aunt.

Zevensprong: A Dutch circle dance with seven different
dance steps.

FURTHER READING

Anne Frank: The Diary of a Young Girl
Edited by Otto H. Frank, Doubleday, 1995.

Hana's Suitcase
Karen Levine, Second Story Press, 2002.

Remember WW II: Kids Who Survived Tell Their Stories
Dorinda Makanaōnalani Nicholson, foreword by
Madeleine K. Albright. National Geographic, 2005.

The World of Anne Frank
Compiled by The Anne Frank House, foreword by
Rabbi Julia Neuberger, PanMacmillan, 2001.

*Fireflies in the Dark: The Story of Friedl Dicker-Brandeis
and the Children of Terezin*
Susan Goldman Rubin, Holiday House, 2000.

ACKNOWLEDGMENTS

Many households in the Netherlands had secrets during the war. Over several years Mies Braal told me about how she and Frans resisted the Nazis. I had not managed to write their story until I stood by Frans Braal's death bed. When I put my hand on his, this book was suddenly fully formed in my head. I want to thank Frans Braal for giving me the inspiration to write this account. I feel privileged to have had the opportunity to do so. My gratitude goes to Mies Braal for providing me with the many details of life in Het Buitenhuis, for editing the story twice and for allowing me to use her archives.

I am also much indebted to Francien and Martin van der Pol, the Braal children, Wim Langendoen, Sabina Kleinsmit, Geert Venhuizen, Mr. v.d. Zee, Mr. Vermeer, Mr. Hanko, Mrs. Steenkist, Mr. Boerma and Mr. H. Ates.

I wish to thank Nan Froman for her thoughtful suggestions and kind editing. Also a huge thank-you goes to writing group members Marylee Banyard and June Johnston, as well as to Nelson's Hume Elementary School enrichment program teacher Lorna Inkster and students Adam, Brittany, Bryce, Danica, Devyn, Dominique, Kelty, Mikki, Rachel B., Rachel S., Sara and Tyler.

With gratitude I acknowledge Adrienne McMillan for information about bomber planes, and the Streekarchief Voorne-Putten & Rozenburg in Holland for information about Second World War resisters working on the island of Voorne.

Thank you also to Kathy Baker and Kevin MacAskill for their technical help as well as to the B.C. Arts Council and the Slocan Valley Arts Council for their grants.

PICTURE CREDITS

All images are courtesy of the Braal family archives except for the following:
Alma archives 23, 30, 38, 57, 62; Canadian Press 69; Canadian Warplane
Heritage Museum 25; Hulton Archive /Getty Images front cover top;
Nederlands Instituut voor Oorlogsdocumentatie 80; Streekarchief Voorne-
Putten & Rozenburg / Jan de Baan 20.

Maps by Leon Grek.